DATE DUE

PLUM PUDDING

for CHRISTMAS

WRITTEN AND ILLUSTRATED BY **Virginia Kahl**

Charles Scribner's Sons   NEW YORK

Copyright 1956 by Virginia Kahl   Printed in the United States of America E-4.66(AJ)

It was just before Christmas and frosty and cold,
And the castle, though drafty, was bright to behold,
For the girls and the Duchess had gathered some holly.
"If your father were here, it could really be jolly."
But in armor complete, with a sword and a shield,
The Duke had gone off to a far battlefield.
He'd galloped away with a wave and a shout;
It was over a year since he'd been about.
He'd promised them jewels and silks and spice,
And an enemy's head (which wasn't so nice).
And Christmas without him would not be so gay,
For everyone missed him since he'd been away—
The Duchess, the cook and his daughters: Clothilde,
Madeleine, Gwendolyn, Jane, and Mathilde,
Caroline, Genevieve, Maude, and Brunhilde,
Willibald, Guinevere, Joan and Gunhilde.

Since they all were so lonely and all were so sad,
The cook cheered them up with a thought that she'd had:
"Why not ask the King if he'd like to dine
With you at Christmas?" They all said, "That's fine."

So they all wrote a note with a few fancy touches:

They sent it right off to the castle nearby
Then waited and waited to hear the reply.

"All right," said the King, "I guess I can come,
If you serve a pudding—and that pudding is plum.
Plums that are purple, plums in a clump,
So that each bumpy lump is a plum that is plump."

"Oh, fine," said the Duchess. "He says he can come
If we serve a pudding—and that pudding is plum.
A plum pudding's easy—it's nothing to bake it,
So let's start at once, and we'll all help you make it."

Now to cook for a king, is a big undertaking;
And too many cooks can spoil anyone's baking.
For Madeleine spilled all the milk on the floor;
Gwendolyn broke all the eggs, and what's more,
Maude threw a handful of nuts at Mathilde;
Jane poured some oil and it soaked poor Clothilde.
Willibald stirred up some very rare spice,
But what she stirred up didn't taste very nice.
Guinevere pinched her left thumb in the door;
Genevieve fell and then started to roar.
Someone tied Caroline up in a sack,
And a jar tumbled down, hitting Joan with a crack.

The Duchess was busy advising Brunhilde,
But no one kept watch on the little Gunhilde.

"Enough!" cried the cook. "Can't you leave me alone?
There's a pudding to make, there's so much to be done.
Don't you know that at Christmas a cook's very busy?
With puddings and pastries and roasts, I'm quite dizzy.
Take a walk—write a note—have a talk—read a book—
Do anything else—but *don't* help me cook!"

It was then that the girls gave a couple of yips.
"Look at Gunhilde—she's licking her lips."
"Gunhilde, Gunhilde, oh, what have you done?"
(She'd eaten the plums and she thought it was fun.)

"Let's see," said the cook,
    "if there are any more."
They looked in the bags
    and behind every door.

They looked in the towers
    and under the stairs.

They hunted alone
    and they hunted in pairs.

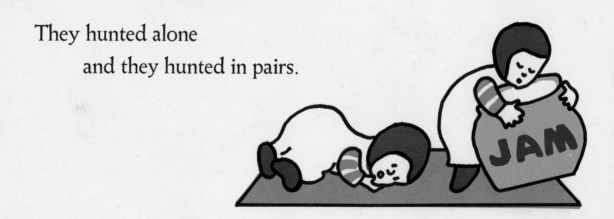

They looked in the crannies
and looked in the nooks;

They looked in the cupboards
and riffled the books.

They looked round the castle,
but when they were done,
They had looked everywhere—
and they hadn't found one!

"We are lost," cried the Duchess,
　　"with Christmas tomorrow!"
"Perhaps," said the cook,
　　"there are some we could borrow."

They sent to the East
　　and they sent to the West—
"Please lend us some plums—
　　we are having a guest.

And we'll give you anything
　　(that's within reason),
But we *must* have some plums,
　　and they're all out of season."

The heralds returned, having been all around,
And they said that there wasn't one plum to be found.

"Now what's to be done? There is no doubt about it,
The King wants his pudding; he won't come without it."

Said the cook, "There's a wizard who's living nearby,
Perhaps he could help us—at least he could try."
So they wended their way to his small lonely cell,
And the Duchess said, "Wizard, oh mix me a spell.
You've powders and herbs, dried wings of a bat,
Magical potions of this and of that,
Henbane and madwort and lizards and such—
Please mix me a spell with your magical touch."

"Now, I can mix silver and I can mix gold.
I can mix spells so you'll never grow old.
Truth powders, love potions, and poisons undreamt—
But plums is a problem I'd never attempt."

"Oh, what's to be done? There is no doubt about it,
The King wants his pudding—he won't come without it."

"Don't feel sad," said the cook. "And let's not be hasty;
If we leave out the plums, it can still be quite tasty."
So they sent off a note to the castle nearby
And waited impatiently for the reply.
But when the note came, the King said, "I object,

For surely you know that this isn't correct.
Now everyone knows, if he isn't too dumb,
That you can't have plum pudding, if you haven't a plum—
Plums that are purple, plums in a clump,
So that each bumpy lump is a plum that is plump."

Then the Duchess said brightly, "I've an idea, you know,
I *could* bake a cake—I'm quite handy with dough."
But the others said, "No, though you're kind to suggest it.
As far as your luck goes, let's not try to test it."

The King hearing this, looked exceedingly glum.
"When I say plum pudding, I want pudding that's plum.
Plum pudding's my favorite, and Christmas without it
Is no Christmas at all—there is no doubt about it.
I don't ask for much, and I don't like to fight,
But I'll cut off your heads if the pudding's not right."

"He'll cut off our heads—though we don't often use 'em,
It will come as a shock when the time comes to lose 'em."

When Christmas arrived a bright beautiful day,
They weren't very bright and they weren't very gay.
        Said the Duchess,
            "I wish that your father were here,
He isn't much help,
            but at least he'd be near."

They climbed to the tower to look for their guest,
And saw the King galloping over the crest.

Then all of them grew
more morose and moroser.
And meantime
the King approached

. . . closer

. . . and closer.

The Duchess remained in the tower until
Another lone figure came over the hill.
And as it came nearer, she looked hard. Of course!
There was the Duke, coming home on his horse!
She ran from the tower in order to meet him,
And all of the girls hurried forward to greet him.

But he looked very sad, and he looked very cold.
"I didn't bring silks and I didn't bring gold.
And I didn't fight. I met one foe, you see,
And he turned out to be just a person like me.
If I cut off his head, it might ruin his figger—
So I just came on home. (Besides, he was bigger.)

"I'm sorry to say that all I brought back
Is a big clump of plump purple plums in a sack."

"Plums in a sack!
        Purple plums in a sack!
They're better than gold,
        and we're glad that you're back."

They rushed to the kitchen
        and called through the door,
"Oh, see what our father's
        brought back from the war!"

"How nice," said the cook,
        "now it's easy to make it.
I'll just add the plums,
        stir it up, and then bake it."

They jumped when they heard
        someone pound
        at the gate.

"Hi," said the King, "I hope I'm not late."

When the pudding came in,
      he said, "Glad I could come,
For I do love a pudding,
      if that pudding is plum—
Plums that are purple,
      plums in a clump,
So that each bumpy lump
      is a plum that is plump."

What a wonderful Christmas,
        with good things to eat,
Boars' heads and pastries and cakes for a treat.
Holly and mistletoe cheered up the gloom
And the Yule log burned brightly to warm up the room.
The girls sang some carols and then sang some more.
"We're happy," they cried. "Father's back from the war!"
The Duke was glad too. "Especially," said he,
"When the person I fight is much bigger than me."

And while they enjoyed it, they firmly agreed
That a Christmas like this is what all people need.
For everyone knows that when Christmastime comes,
There should always be pudding with plenty of plums,
Plums that are purple, plums in a clump,
So that each bumpy lump is a plum that is plump.